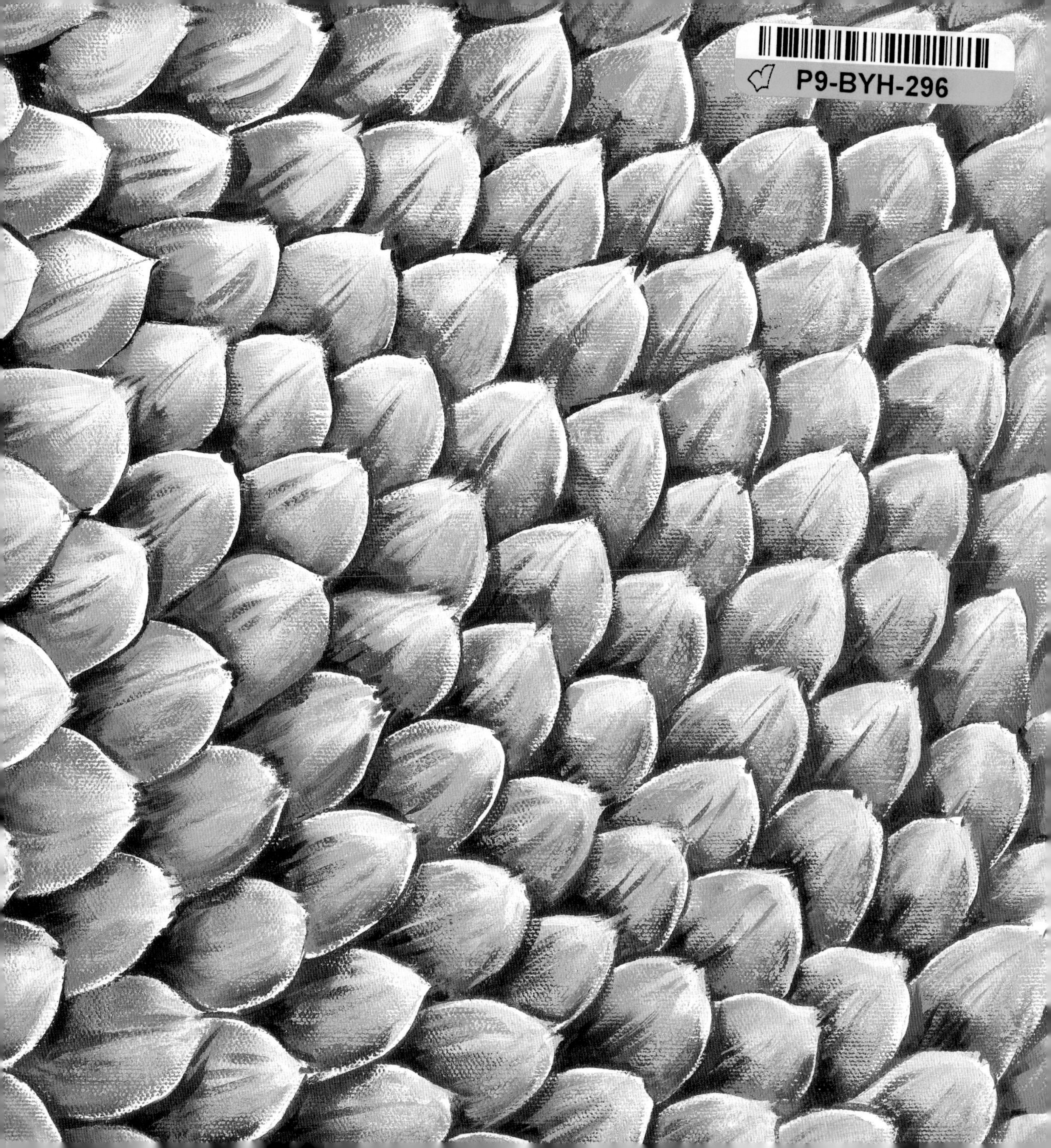

Roly Poly Pangolin

Anna Dewdney

VIKING
An Imprint of Penguin Group (USA) Inc.

Roly Poly, very small,
doesn't like new things at all.

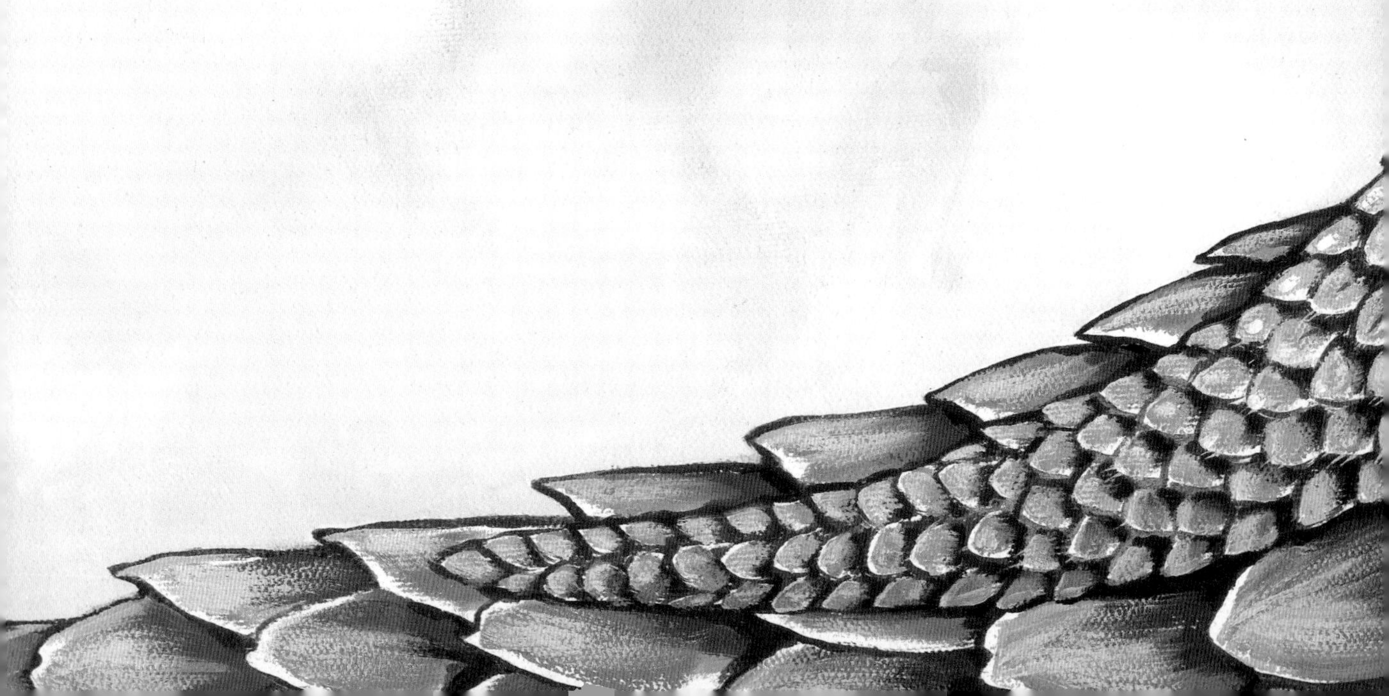

What if something out there **bites?**
Roly Poly holds on tight.

Roly Poly, very small,
doesn't like new things at all.

What's for dinner? Ants and slugs.
Roly Poly won't touch bugs.

Roly Poly, very small,
doesn't like new things at all.

Someone furry wants to play.
Roly Poly runs away.

Roly Poly, very small,
doesn't like new things at all.

Rustle! Snap!
What can it be?
Roly does not want to see.

Roly Poly, very small,
hears a teeny tiny call.

Scary monster sounds?
Oh no!

Roly Poly,

GO GO GO!

Roly Poly, very small,

stubs his toe and starts to **fall.**

Now the world is upside down.

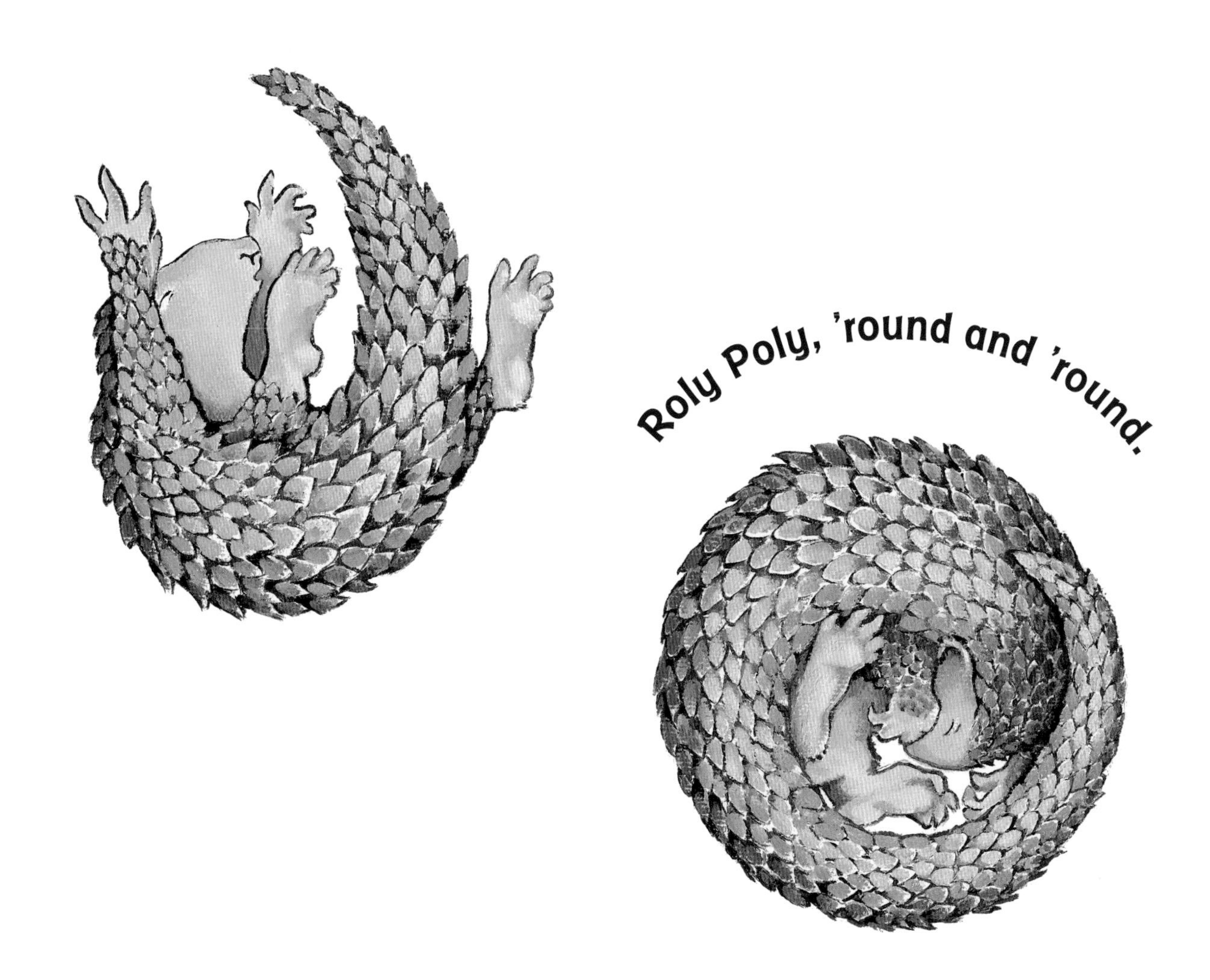

Roly Poly, ’round and ’round.

Roly Poly, very small,
tucks up tight into a ball.
Rumpty-bumpty down the hill . . .

Roly Poly, very still.

Roly Poly,
very small,
all alone inside his ball.

The world's outside
but he's within—
Roly Poly Pangolin.

Roly Poly, very small,
hears another tiny call,
opens eyes a **teensy** crack . . .

Another ball

is peeking back!

Roly Poly, very small,

not so frightened, after all.

Sometimes new things can be **fun**
when you're not the only one.

Roly Poly, very small,
feeling better, feeling tall.
So much to see, so much to do . . .

So much nicer when it's two!

PANGOLINS are an endangered species. Their habitat is disappearing quickly, and their greatest enemy is mankind.

Pangolins can be found in Africa, India, China, and Southeast Asia. They have furry tummies and no teeth, and they protect themselves by rolling into tight balls so that they are completely covered by their scales. Pangolins are mammals and have only one baby at a time . . . and the baby often gets around by riding on Mama's tail!

For more information on pangolins and how you can help them, please visit Anna's Web site: www.annadewdney.com. A portion of the proceeds of this book will go to the Pangolin Conservation Program at Cuc Phuong National Park in Vietnam and the research going on there to save the pangolin.

For Reed

VIKING
Published by Penguin Group
Penguin Young Readers Group, 345 Hudson Street, New York, New York 10014, U.S.A.
Penguin Group (Canada), 90 Eglinton Avenue East, Suite 700, Toronto, Ontario, Canada M4P 2Y3 (a division of Pearson Penguin Canada Inc.)
Penguin Books Ltd, 80 Strand, London WC2R 0RL, England
Penguin Ireland, 25 St Stephen's Green, Dublin 2, Ireland (a division of Penguin Books Ltd)
Penguin Group (Australia), 250 Camberwell Road, Camberwell, Victoria 3124, Australia (a division of Pearson Australia Group Pty Ltd)
Penguin Books India Pvt Ltd, 11 Community Centre, Panchsheel Park, New Delhi - 110 017, India
Penguin Group (NZ), 67 Apollo Drive, Rosedale, North Shore 0745, Auckland, New Zealand (a division of Pearson New Zealand Ltd.)
Penguin Books (South Africa) (Pty) Ltd, 24 Sturdee Avenue, Rosebank, Johannesburg 2196, South Africa

Penguin Books Ltd, Registered Offices: 80 Strand, London WC2R 0RL, England

First published in 2010 by Viking, a division of Penguin Young Readers Group

1 3 5 7 9 10 8 6 4 2

LIBRARY OF CONGRESS CATALOGING-IN-PUBLICATION DATA
Dewdney, Anna.
Roly Poly pangolin / by Anna Dewdney.
p. cm.
Summary: Roly Poly, a pangolin, is shy and afraid of new things until he discovers that some new experiences are not bad at all.
ISBN 978-0-670-01160-5 (hardcover)
Special Markets ISBN 978-0-670-01393-7 Not for resale
[1. Stories in rhyme. 2. Pangolins—Fiction. 3. Timidity—Fiction.] I. Title.
PZ8.3.D498Ro 2010 [E]—dc22 2009022468

Manufactured in China • Set in Badger • Book design by Sam Kim

This Imagination Library edition is published by Penguin Group (USA), a Pearson company, exclusively for Dolly Parton's Imagination Library, a not-for-profit program designed to inspire a love of reading and learning, sponsored in part by The Dollywood Foundation. Penguin's trade editions of this work are available wherever books are sold.

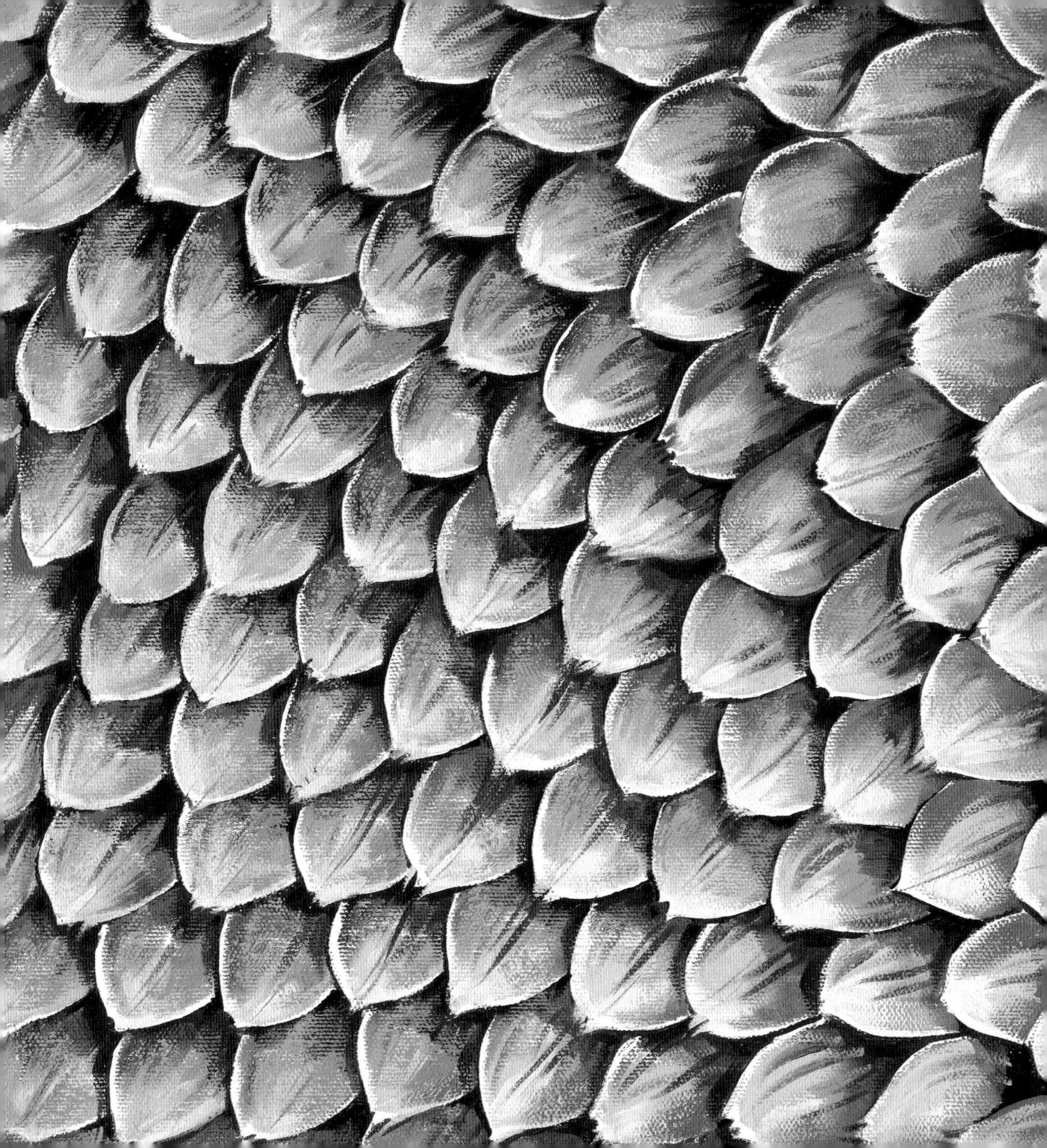